HEARTS OF WOOD

William Kotzwinkle

❀✳❀✳❀✳❀✳❀✳❀✳❀✳❀✳❀✳❀✳❀

HEARTS
OF WOOD

❀✳❀✳❀✳❀✳❀✳❀✳❀✳❀✳❀✳❀✳❀

AND OTHER TIMELESS TALES

illustrated by Joe Servello

David R. Godine · Publisher

BOSTON

First edition published in 1986 by
DAVID R. GODINE, PUBLISHER, INC.
Horticultural Hall
300 Massachusetts Avenue
Boston, Massachusetts 02115

Library of Congress Cataloging in Publication Data
Kotzwinkle, William.
Hearts of wood.
Summary: A collection of fairy tales including a
wooden carousel that comes alive through the magic of
a troll, and a butterfly catcher who dreams he becomes
a butterfly.
1. Fairy tales—United States.   2. Children's
stories, American. [1. Fairy tales.   2. Short
stories]   I. Servello, Joe, ill.   II. Title.
PZ8.K84He   1986   [Fic]   86-45539
ISBN 0-87923-648-5

FIRST EDITION
Printed in the United States of America

CONTENTS

HEARTS
OF WOOD

"Take a ride, step right up, we'll be starting in a minute." He wore a captain's cap, though he had no ship. He was Captain of the Carousel, and he loved its animals as if they were real and living creatures. He kept them painted and brightly polished, and oiled their bridles and stirrups every morning.

"There you go, my fine Arabian steed, here's a rider for you, show him your fire." And he placed the children on the ponies and in the coaches, proud of every one of the animals, and their spirited performance. "Who dances like my panda? Who leaps like my kangaroo? It's a grand carousel, ladies and gentlemen, it turns by day, every day, but it does not turn by night. So ride 'er while you can, thank you ma'am, there's a fine steed for you . . ."

He helped all the people on, some to the ponies, some to the panda. Gentlemen frequently rode the panda, in a dignified manner.

"Now she's starting, hold on fast." The Captain threw the lever and, at the center of the turning wheel, the black bear thumped his drum. The monkey banged his cymbals and away the ponies went, up and down, round and round. "Ah, what music," said the Captain. "I never tire of the way my animals play." He sat in his rickety chair and watched the carousel turn, nodding his head with the melody and tapping his old boot to the time. "That's the song that keeps me well," he said. "And this is the sight that keeps me young." He smiled as the bright frogs wheeled by, pulling their coach full of children. "A carousel is one of the secrets of life," he said to anyone who'd listen, but no one did—except perhaps the animals.

Did the panda softly speak to the kangaroo?

"Not a word, not a peep, not a sound from any of them," said the Captain, "for their throats are made of wood, but they never tire, they can run forever. That is the nature of a carousel."

So he watched, and hummed, and sometimes sang to the carousel tune, as the great wheel turned, flags waving. And when the ride ended, he came forward again, to help people off, and to praise his animals. "You gave them all a wonderful ride, my friends, one they'll not forget." Day ran on, and the sun, which circles slowly, sank at last. The Captain stopped the wheel and closed his ticket box. Then he went among the animals and polished them with a cloth, and patted their wooden necks. "What a splendid frog. I've never seen your like. And oh my pretty little dragon." She was petite, the lady-dragon who pulled the dainty coach, and her long eyelashes were brightly painted, while her tail was gaily decorated, inlaid with bits of colored glass. "Rest now, you've ridden hard. Rest and dream, for you do not turn by night."

The Captain folded his rickety chair, and walked down the path, into the shadows of the evening. The park grew still. The squirrels retired to their trees, and the birds to their nests. Only the white goose was awake, but she was drifting toward sleep, upon the lake. The moon appeared through the branches, and rose, in its own slow arc, until it had filled the park with silvery light, which shone upon the ponies' hooves, over at the carousel.

Now soft voices could be heard, the frogs gruffly speaking. "Bound in a ring," said one in a plumed wooden hat. "How I'd like to jump in a lake, just once. For after all, I am a frog."

"Yes," said his associate, a frog in a gorgeously carved cape and musketeer's boots. "Yes, that would be lovely, to sing and splash."

They listened in their wooden stillness to the other frogs, the wet, green ones down at the lake, who sang to each other and to the moon. And deep longing filled the wooden hearts of the wooden frogs.

"Don't go stirring up wooden heads," said the black bear, at the center of the wheel. He was content, he loved his drum. "We are wooden," he said, "and we belong right where we are, attached to the turning wheel."

"The frogs are right," said the Arabian pony, a brilliant creature of passionate eyes, whose silvery hooves were made more splendid by the moon. "I would love to gallop through the fields." And he gazed toward those open spaces on which his eyes were ever fixed.

"Foolishness," snapped the black bear.

"Well," said the monkey, "I wouldn't mind leading a small parade down the avenue." And his wooden head seemed to nod, ever so slightly, toward that tempting street he saw each day, when the carousel turned toward the edge of the park.

"We may dream," said the panda. "But who of us can move the lever by himself? And even if we could set the wheel turning, we'd only circle, as always, in a ring."

"A moonlight ride then!" said the Arabian pony. "Black Bear, you are close to the switch, reach with your drumstick."

"Wooden arms do not reach."

"Monkey," said the Arabian pony, "you are quick and agile. Grip the lever with those clever hands of yours."

And the monkey tried, willing from deep within his wooden frame. His wooden fingers itched, his wooden eyes beseeched the night to set him free, but the night passed on, unheeding. And the carousel stayed still, and was that way at morning, with dew upon the animals' bright costumes.

The Captain arrived, and bid them all good day. He polished the brass ring, and swept the wooden floor, and told the animals, as he always did, that they were the finest, the best. And when the crowds began to come, the animals all were shining, from polish and pride. "Step right up and ride, there's nothing like turning in the morning, through the new-born light."

And the businessmen with their briefcases rode the panda in a dignified manner, and the carousel turned on through the day; hundreds of rides were taken, and the brass ring was won. The wooden creatures obeyed, frogs pulling, kangaroo hopping, and ponies gliding up and down. "They're a steady bunch," said the Captain. "They do as they are told."

At evening he folded his chair again, and bid them all goodnight. "Rest up," he said. "You've ridden many miles. As for me, I will go home to bed and dream of you. For that is what I dream each night, of this carousel turning."

They watched as his familiar form became a shadow, disappearing slowly down the path. And then the frogs spoke up. "I am a prince," said one. "Look at my hat, my sword, my golden braid. Surely I should be allowed to jump in the lake."

"A prince?" said the black bear. "You're a block of wood."

The frog mumbled into his bright vest about the thickness of the black bear's head. *But he's right,* thought the frog, *I'm just a lifeless piece of oak. And yet, and yet . . .*

He listened to the wet green frogs splashing and singing to the moon, as it rose through the trees.

I would love to jump into the lake.

He tried to turn within the carriage reins, but it was a hopeless wish. He was fixed, forever, where he stood. And fixed beside him was the other frog, in similar design, both their eyes gazing at the moonstruck lake.

The lake was calm; the goose, floating with her neck curled round and down, drifted slowly off to sleep. The wet green frogs, scattered all along the edges of the lake, croaked and sang, serenading the moon and creating that peculiar magic of water by night. How deep their song went is hard to say, but eventually a disturbance began in the thick mud of the bank.

The mud heaved, and a head emerged, features indiscernible at first. "Awful mess, this," said a gravelly voice, as two knobby hands wiped away the mud. Two pointed ears now showed clear, and then a pair of enormous eyes, set in a knobby head. ". . . must have taken a wrong turning, don't recognize a thing," said the creature, who was, in fact, a tunnel troll.

He splashed some water on himself. "Mud quite unexpected. Hoping for sand, possibly grass." He washed himself off, revealing a countenance remarkable for its monstrosity. He bent over the water again and, catching sight of his reflection in the moonlight, remarked, "Handsome devil. A great waste, hiding features like these in a tunnel. However, that is the nature of the beast."

He looked around, trying to discern his whereabouts, but seeing no familiar landmark, he questioned the wet green frogs. "Looking for the Trolls' Convention. Big field? Lots of rock or something?" The wet green frogs gazed suspiciously at him, only their eyes showing, the rest of their bodies dangling below the surface of the water.

"Hmmmm, not much help from this crowd," said the troll.

And he set off up the hill. "Some sort of tent there. Must be the place."

But it was not the place. It was the carousel. The troll had never seen one before, and was quite taken with the silver beauty of the ponies' hooves as he approached. "I say there, can you tell me—" And he explained all about the Trolls' Convention, for which he'd tunneled halfway round the world.

He received no answer.

"Come, come," said the troll, "don't be dazzled by my beauty, speak up." He paced around them, and only gradually did he realize that he was talking, essentially, to trees. "Wood," he said, knocking on the black bear's head. "Well, well . . ."

He scratched his own head awhile, trying to recall the correct enchantment for trees, the one that permitted them to speak. "Is it Digabow or Mundering Magglefump? Let me try one and see . . ."

He tried Digabow and a pothole opened beneath his feet, submerging him in mud again. ". . . not Digabow," he said, crawling up out of the ground and brushing himself off. "Then it has to be Mundering Magglefump, or I'm not a licensed magician."

He made the appropriate gesture and a torrent of hailstones fell upon him with great force, rendering his knobby head still more knobby. Taking cover beneath the roof of the carousel, he pondered more deeply. ". . . not Digabow and not Mundering M. Must be, has to be, Kighfly Nabbletoes." He took a protected position in case more hail or something should manifest, and then made the gestures of Kighfly Nabbletoes, whispering, *Let the solemn wood speak . . .*"

"I'm a prince of frogs . . ."

"Let's go for a gallop!"

". . . take a swim!"

". . . have a parade!"

Everyone spoke at once, and the troll could get very little sense out of anyone. Did they know where the Trolls' Convention was to be held? No. Did they know who *might* know? No. Did they have any suggestions for him? Yes.

"Have a parade!"

". . . go for a gallop!"

"Quiet," said the troll, "I heard you the first time."

He circled slowly round the carousel, looking at each of the ponies, all of whom whinnied and talked of galloping. The frogs carried on about swimming, and the kangaroo indicated that she wanted to hop down the lane. But the troll was not about to work that kind of magic, which would require a spell to set trees walking. "Big stuff," he said to himself. "Liable to result in all sorts of complications."

"*But I thought,*" said a quiet voice, "*you are a licensed magician.*"

The troll looked around, and saw the petite lady-dragon. Her soulful eyes gazed at him, and her lovely twinkling tail seemed made of softest moonlight. He'd seen dragons before, naturally, for an inhabitant of the deep earth will encounter them now and then. But they were usually a scaly, fire-breathing, sulphurous-smelling lot; not like this adorable creature, who was so smooth, so refined, so brightly painted.

"Well, of course I am a magician. But you see, I'm busy tonight. On my way to the big convention. Important matters to be voted on, shall there be a major earthquake, will a tidal wave be called for, that sort of thing."

"I see," said the dragon softly. Her jeweled tail ceased to shine, for the troll's shadow had fallen across it. Noticing this, he quickly stepped aside.

"Sorry, didn't mean to block your moonlight. Moonlight, most important, can't have enough of it. Well, I suppose I'd better be moving on."

But he didn't move. The little dragon's eyes were upon him, and her painted gaze was remarkable, with a beauty that confused him, upset him, made him stumble on the lever that set the carousel turning.

Black Bear beat his drum, the monkey banged his cymbals. The inner gears were clicking, whirring, spinning, and all the animals were going up and down.

"A midnight moonlight ride!" cried the Arabian pony.

"What a different feeling, to be turning in the dark," said the panda. "I see the whole night sky."

"The lake!" cried the wooden frogs, as they saw it all pass before them, with its coves and moonlit lily pads.

"And lamps are lit, all around the park," said the monkey. "And look, the street is lit, it goes forever in the dark!" He looked down it, down the long ribbon of pave, hung with lights. Ah, could a monkey but march there with his cymbals clanging . . .

The troll, who'd fallen to the floor of the carousel, was clinging to the kangaroo, as the carousel turned; up and down he bounced as the kangaroo hopped. "I say, I say . . ."

"Ride in *my* carriage," said the dragon softly.

The troll regained his balance, and staggered back toward the little dragon. "This thing always goes round and round? Just like this?"

"Round and round," said the dragon, her tail blinking and winking as the carousel raced beneath the moon.

"Most amazing," said the troll, gazing out at the trees that floated past. He knew all things have their wheel—the earth, the moon, the sun, all turning, all wheeling, forever, and it was magic, of course, the highest magic. For what had set them wheeling? A troll reflects upon such matters as he tunnels, even as he sleeps.

"I am most impressed by this object on which we ride," he

said. "Its motion seems to me to be a guide to higher things, to deeper matters, to things, in short, which are my specialty. I shall have to transport this object, at once, to the Trolls' Convention."

"Do it, do it!" cried the Arabian pony, galloping close by. "My spirit longs to roam!"

"It will require a formidable piece of work," said the troll.

"I know you are up to the job," said the dragon.

"Yes," said the panda, "we all know that."

"Well," said the troll, "I have caused boulders to bounce."

"Can a carousel require much more?" asked the kangaroo, who was herself bouncing all the time, up and down.

"Give me a moment," said the troll. "I must collect my spells."

He stepped next to the black bear's beating drum. "Play on, my good fellow, for such incessant rhythm is conducive to magical atmosphere."

"I play," said the black bear. "I play on and on. Beat, beat, beating—"

"Yes, without commentary, please," said the troll. "I must plunge myself into intense thought."

And so he did, closing his eyes and recalling to mind the peculiarly shaped figures from the ancient Grimoire of the Trolls—a book of obscure magical acts known to every troll who has studied in the great caverns. The figures came clearer in his mind, colored by mental powders of a lovely hue. Presently the animals of the carousel saw a powdery cloud forming around the troll's body, shot through with delicate lights of gold and silver and a deep rich blue.

"Isn't he handsome," said the lady dragon, admiring the gaily cloaked troll.

"Handsome, no," said the wooden frogs. "*We* are handsome. But he is certainly causing a strange substance to appear."

The powdery cloud surrounded him now, and he moved his hands through it, shaping it into a long, cylindrical form. The animals saw a snake's head suddenly appear, with diamond eyes and a flickering tongue of fire. It turned, and gazed at the lady dragon. "*Cousin,*" it hissed, and the dragon answered in a tongue the other carousel animals had never heard her use before.

"Truly," said the frogs, "this is a mysterious night."

The snake wrapped itself round the troll, and as the carousel came by the lake, the troll stepped off and gazed at it. "I skry in the spirit vision. I call upon Bilfares, of the waters."

From the shore of the lake, a demon toad appeared, eyes flashing an awesome light. The wet green frogs dove away in fright as the fearful creature looked around. "I am Bilfares," it said, hopping up through the grass to the carousel. "Why have I been summoned?"

"Lifting a carousel, transporting same," said the troll. He unwound the brightly colored serpent from his shoulders and directed it to encircle the carousel. This it did, lengthening its form until it was wound around the base of the carousel like a belt.

"Now," said the troll, "my magic is bound, and protected. Bilfares old chap, what I need from you is a lift. Climb under the carousel like a good demon, and hop us off into the night. I'm traveling to the Trolls' Convention."

"Infernal amount of luggage," grumbled Bilfares, but he headed under the carousel anyway, for he was bound by the power of the Grimoire, ancient Book of Spells.

In the next moment, the animals felt their carousel rising, as Bilfares took a great supernatural hop into the air, the carousel borne on his powerful shoulders. It shuddered and creaked, but the serpent of the Grimoire held it fast, and kept it from flying apart.

The carousel sailed over the trees, music still playing, animals turning.

"We're flying!" cried the Arabian pony. "My hooves touch the sky!"

They sailed beyond the park, and turned above the bright avenue. The monkey banged his cymbals joyously, as they passed the street lamps in their flight.

The first long hop of Bilfares ended in Central Square, where he came down with a gentle glide in the middle of the traffic circle. "Hop along, that's a good fellow," said the troll, and Bilfares lifted the carousel in the air again, over the monument of Columbus, who pointed the way with a stony arm.

Bilfares climbed, his second hop greater than his first, his voice echoing beneath the hub of the carousel. "I can leap to the moon!"

"Let's not overdo it, old boy," said the troll, calling down through the floor of the carousel. "The Convention is quite far enough."

"I'm made for greater things."

"Yes, certainly you are. Now, steady on, trollward."

Bilfares contained himself within the atmosphere of earth, though demons such as he are capable of flight to other worlds, and dimensions far removed. But he was bound by the Grimoire, and the carousel was bound by the serpent, which shone around it like a girdle of silver now, and hummed with a vibrant noise.

The carousel passed beyond the city, and over the river, and Bilfares came down just at the shore, his webbed feet sinking deep in the mud. But he balanced the carousel on his powerful back and leapt once again. "Why am I exerting myself this way? I could dump them all in a hole in the ground. I could hear them crack and break apart. In fact, I think I shall, for I'm an awful character." His eyes were suddenly blood-red, and his poisonous warts were shining. He looked for a place below, on which to shatter the carousel.

"Yes, there's a spot, a granite ledge, on which they'll break like twigs. And I shall swell with laughter, evil toad that I am, wholly without redeeming qualities."

He arched his shoulder, letting the carousel slide. The wooden frogs suddenly found themselves looking straight down into dizzying depths. The Arabian pony felt his stirrups flop sideways, and saw the earth go pitching. And the troll went sliding, hands scratching frantically at the floor of the carousel; he knocked his head on silver hooves, got kicked in the back by the kangaroo, and found himself tumbling toward the edge. He lashed out, grabbing the dragon's bridle, from which he dangled.

"Bilfares, you treacherous brute!"

Bilfares readied himself to chuck the whole crowd; but the bear still beat his drum, and the music of the carousel played, a tune very old, of a specially enchanting kind; and woven within in were the sounds of children's voices, all those who'd ridden the wooden animals and left their delighted laughter in the tune. Bilfares found himself listening, and nodded. "Yes, just the sort of music I hate." He lifted one mighty leg, his webbed appendage spreading, in order to flick the carousel end-over-end.

The voice of the Grimoire, ancient Book of Spells, sounded in the air. "Bilfares, foul toad, carry on as directed, or the invisible force of the Grimoire will lay you low."

And the Grimoire sent a vision to Bilfares, of himself turned into a wad of old chewing gum, stuck on a shoe for the next two thousand years.

"Only joking," said Bilfares, grinning toadishly. He righted the carousel and glided down gently to the granite ledge. The troll sighted off the end of the carousel, toward a field far in the distance, where flickering fairy lights burned. "The Convention!" he cried. "One more leap, and we'll be there!"

Bilfares leapt, and they were there, coming down in a large open field whose edges were bounded by a circle of rock. Trolls had gathered, hundreds of them, and they'd brought a host of attendant elementals—elves, gnomes, sylphs, and water nixies. But no one had brought a carousel and it made a tremendous impression.

"It turns, like the zoidion!"

"Like the stars . . ."

". . . the sun . . ."

". . . the moon . . ."

And the trolls all gathered around it, fascinated by its movement and beauty. The tunneling troll gave a speech, about how he'd found it, and then showed everyone how to ride it. "Climb on, hold tight. It turns by day and night." He stationed himself beside the little dragon, and indicated that the fairies and elves could fit comfortably in her carriage. The trolls, he made clear, should feel free to ride on the ponies and the panda and the kangaroo.

"Hurrah!"

"We're on our way!"

"This pony—is *mine*."

"Can't we both ride?"

"Yes, if you get on back, *I* need to see."

And so the trolls all clambered aboard, some riding, others just holding to the iron poles. One stuck his head between the monkey's cymbals just as they clanged shut. "I say, have you tried this!" He signaled to the others, and they lined up, to have their heads clanged.

The black bear beat his drum and the carousel turned, trolls going up and down, shouting, laughing, and waving their long bony arms about. The fairies flew here and there, and lit the carousel with hundreds of tiny lanterns. And so it all turned, on through the night, and everyone forgot about the earthquake they'd been planning, and the tidal wave.

"Best not to have a quake," said the Lord of Trolls. "We don't want to upset this thing we're riding on. It has a delicate mechanism."

So the earthquake was officially scratched from the program. In its place was inserted Frequent Carousel Riding. But one of the fairies, a mischievous sort skilled in tree magic, worked through the night to cast an age-old spell. While the trolls rode around, shouting and yelling, she worked with wand and chant, and suddenly—the Arabian pony leapt from the carousel, his silver hooves shining, his body free.

"I'm galloping! I'm alive! I'm a true Arabian pony!"

He pranced and bucked and the troll on his back was tossed in the bushes. The other ponies followed, their nostrils steaming, their breath real. "We're free!" they cried, and they were, galloping in every direction, with troll riders hanging on precariously, half in the saddle and half out.

"Parade time," said the monkey, and he stepped from the carousel to begin his march, through the moonlit field, with the black bear right behind him. "So now," said the black bear, "we shall wander the wide earth. Is it what we want?"

"Of course it's what we want," said the monkey, and several trolls seemed to want it too, for they lined up in the parade, marching away, into the night.

The Lord of Trolls rode the kangaroo. "You shall be the resident animal in my court," he said. "We shall spend much time hopping about. I'll send important letters in your pouch."

The wooden panda climbed carefully down, and turned to the east. "I must travel to Tibet, to the groves of bamboo."

"But Tibet is terribly far off," said the dozen elves who'd climbed on his back.

"Nonetheless, I must go there or starve."

"Then we'll go with you," they said, "to help you find your way."

And soon they were only shadows, disappearing in the moon-lit field. The magic serpent of the Grimoire faded too, for it was no longer needed to bind the animals safely in a ring.

As for the wooden frogs, they were wooden no longer. "The nearest pond, please, where is it?"

"Through that grove of trees," said the water nixies, and they led the frogs away, and soon there was a joyous sound of splashing and diving.

The last ones on the carousel were the tunneling troll and the lady dragon. She'd come to life and he'd fallen on his knobby knees before her. "You must be mine, forever. I cannot live without you."

"Then let us be off together," she said, "before the spell is broken. For one never knows if fairy magic lasts."

They crossed the field, and her dragon tail shone, glittering more beautifully than ever; and the tunneling troll felt his gnarled heart, centuries old, filling with joy. I'll show her the tunnels of the world, and we shall boat upon hidden streams to lakes that no one knows, in the silence of the deep. There, in those dark remote places, far from the madness of things, she will feel the supreme solitude of the inner earth. "Ah, the stillness," he cried, "you will be unable to comprehend its glory, there in the core. But you will be happy, my dear, and so shall I, happier than any troll who ever lived."

And they disappeared, beneath a stone, into the caverns.

The carousel stood empty in the field—all its animals gone.

"It's not the same without them, is it," said the remaining trolls, who hung dully to its iron poles, as it circled slowly round.

"No, the animals were the life and beauty of the thing."

And one by one they stepped down from it, and drifted on their way.

"Well," said Bilfares the toad, "if there's no further work for me—"

The voice of the Grimoire spoke in the dark: "Return the wheel from whence it came. The Grimoire leaves no loose ends."

"Very well," said Bilfares, but in his heart he vowed he'd pay back the tunneling troll who'd caused him to be used like a common mule. "Very well," he said, lifting the carousel aloft. *But I'll remember this night, tunneling troll. And Bilfares is not without magic of his own.*

He placed the carousel down in the park, shortly before dawn, and when the Captain came round at seven to start his day, he found it there—stripped, nothing left but the empty coaches. He ran forward, trembling all over. "My animals! My dear friends!" He picked up the frogs' empty harness, and ran it through his fingers. "Frogs," he said softly, "where are you?"

He clung to an empty pole, where once a pony had been. His hands were still shaking, and his cheeks were wet with tears. "Gone, all gone," he cried, as he staggered from pole to pole. "It's the sorriest looking carousel I've ever seen." He threw the lever. "There's music, but no black bear to beat the drum, no monkey to bang the cymbals."

When the businessmen came by with their briefcases, there was no panda on which to ride in a dignified way. When the children came, there were poles but no ponies, and hanging onto a pole is not much fun, when you are used to riding an Arabian steed. The Captain put on a few milk crates, and an old soap box, but by no stretch of the imagination were they prancing ponies. Some people jeered, and a squirrel hurled a nut at him.

Why, he asked himself, did they leave me? Didn't I treat

them well? I kept their paint brand new, I oiled their harness straps.

At the end of day, not a single ticket had been sold. The Captain sat in his rickety chair and stared dully at the ground. "The rent will fall due and I'll not have it." He looked up at a squirrel in a nearby tree. "It's expensive to rent space in the park, you know." The squirrel threw a nut at him.

Some children came by, and stared at the empty carousel. The Captain said, "You can ride in the frogs' coach."

"There are no frogs pulling it," said the children.

"No," said the Captain, "I know."

"Were there *ever* any frogs pulling it?"

"Once there were splendid frogs pulling it, in cloaks and bright caps."

"Where are they now?"

"They vanished in the night. Perhaps they were stolen. Or maybe they strayed away."

The Captain stood, and shook his head. He was finished as a master of the carousel. He picked up his lunch pail and shuffled down the path. He'd thought that he was somebody, and he'd called himself Captain, but without his carousel he was just an old man.

"Captain!" called the children.

The sun was setting. He walked into the last rays of the day, and hung his captain's hat on a tree, near the path to the carousel. Without it he seemed to grow suddenly smaller, and he stepped into the shadows of evening.

My ponies, he said to himself. My panda. And he felt them in his heart, going round. The black bear beat his drum there, and there the monkey clanged his cymbals. The frogs pulled the coach, the kangaroo hopped, and all of it went round, tiny and bright, in the chambers of the Captain's heart. He heard the music all through his nerves, at first quite loud and clear.

But then it began to fade, and fading too was the carousel's turning in his heart.

"The carousel is life," he said, and knew that his was ended. He fell on the path, with his head near the pond, where the white goose swam. The great bird lifted her head and cried, "Foolish animals! Your master is dying without you!"

". . . dying without you . . . dying without you," echoed the wet green frogs in the water.

The park was still, only the voices of the birds and the frogs sounding in the cool shadows. But then there came the sound of hoofbeats, pounding across the field. And the Arabian pony galloped into view, the other ponies right behind him. Their silver hooves were shining, their manes tossing wildly, and they leapt with a great clatter onto the carousel, and took their places.

A drum sounded, and cymbals clanged, and the monkey and the black bear marched up the street. "We're coming!" said the monkey. And to himself he thought, *I've had my parade, and a good one too. Shall I ever have another?* But he could not let the Captain die.

He and the black bear climbed onto the carousel and took their places at the center of the wheel.

The kangaroo came hopping by, bearing the Lord of Trolls, who lifted the unconscious Captain up and carried him to his rickety chair. "There," said the Lord of Trolls, "that's where he belongs."

"And here's where I belong," said the kangaroo, leaping onto the wheel.

The frogs came, their clothes all wet, and lily pads trailing from their ears. "Swimming's alright," said one, "but it ruins the costume, you see."

"Yes," said the other, "and we must look spiffy, you know." But they took a last look at the lake, and what was in their eyes? But when they looked at the Captain slumped in his rickety chair, they stepped into their bridles.

The panda was the last to come, waddling up the path. "Tibet is much too far," he said. "My paws are terribly sore." He climbed onto the wheel in a dignified manner, and took his position at the pole.

"But where is our dragon?" asked the monkey.

*　　*　　*

She was in the caverns of the earth, where the stillness is profound. The tunnel troll was beside her, a lantern in his hand. But the dragon suddenly turned. "I'm being called back," she said. "I feel the fairy magic ending."

"No!" cried the troll. "I have different magic we can use."

"Too late," she said, "the others are all in place. I can feel them, and you and I, dear troll, cannot alter what the wheel has decreed."

Her form was changing before him, turning to powdery light, and he knew she was about to be transported, back to her place on the carousel. He grabbed her arm, and the powerful pull of the wheel pulled him too, out of the caverns of the earth and across the night sky. They sailed quickly, sharing a final embrace. "Oh troll," she said, "how shall I live without you!"

The troll was mad with grief, and could only hold her tight, as they decended down toward the park.

"Ah ha," said Bilfares, springing from the waters of the lake. "Now, while the troll is confused, I shall strike." He hopped into the moonlight, following them, and as they landed on the carousel, Bilfares worked his spell.

His webbed fingers gestured, his power spat forth. The lady-dragon was taking her place on the wheel, and the troll was sobbing a last kiss upon her cheek, as he watched her turn to wood.

The spell of Bilfares fell: the troll felt his body stiffen all over, felt his skin grow hard. He too was turned to wood, a painted figure on the carousel, his lips fixed forever to his beloved's cheek.

My deepest wish has been granted, he said. You are mine for eternity.

Troll, dear troll, said the dragon softly.

And when the Captain woke in his chair, his carousel was turning. "Ah," he said, "It must have been a dream, that's all! For here are all my friends. But who," he cried, gazing at the wooden troll, "is that?"

I am love, said the troll.

THE DREAM OF CHUANG

※❖※❖※❖※❖※❖※❖※❖※❖

C HUANG WAS A butterfly collector. Each day he roamed the hills and fields with his net, chasing the beautiful creatures who fluttered among the flowers. He brought each captured beauty back to his shop, where he pressed them in paper, or put them in glass boxes, and sold them to customers from near and far. He made a small living, and was happy.

Each night, after the day's work was done and supper was ended, Chuang said to his wife, "I will now lay my humble self into bed, and sleep." And each night, he passed into a dark, dreamless place. When other people told of their dreams, he could only nod his head and wonder. He never had a single dream—only a dark place about which he could remember nothing.

In this way did he pass the years—through the bright hills and fields by day, pursuing the tiny navigators of the breeze, and into the darkness at night, where nothing of Chuang existed, except an occasional snore, so loud it woke him with alarm. Then he would go to the window and look at the moon, across which the wild duck flew, beyond the nets of men.

· 31 ·

One afternoon, in the field called Happiest Meadow, Chuang was racing with his long-handled net. This net was woven of most delicate fiber, so the fragile wings of his prey would not be damaged in the capture. He was chasing a magnificent specimen, the finest he had ever seen. Its wings were large and golden, and traced upon them in violet dust were two radiant dragon's eyes, which seemed to blink and wink as the wings worked in the wind.

Chuang was enraptured. It must have been a king of butterflies, for it eluded him with ease, seemed to be teasing him, on and on, from flower to flower in Happiest Meadow. With each failing sweep of the net, silk threads just missing the elegant wings, Chuang's heart grew more determined to possess forever this most perfect treasure.

Across Happiest Meadow they went, through thicket and glen, Chuang waving his net, the grand butterfly masterfully dodging it. Finally, running blindly forward, seeing not the ground, but only the flickering sun-wings in the air, Chuang's feet sank into mud. He stopped on the edge of the meadow lake, and watched his precious prey fly far out over the water, and land in the middle of the lake, upon a floating lotus.

"What is my miserable life worth?" reflected Chuang, and deciding it was dark emptiness without the little jewel sitting so serenely beyond him on the lotus, he plunged forward through the water.

He sank in to his knees, his stomach, his chest, his chin. With only his head above water, he splashed forward, holding his net in the air. The fish and turtles marveled. The bottom of the lake fell away. "I am sinking over my worthless head," observed Chuang, and began to swim, one-armed through the water, keeping his net held high, like a battle banner.

The butterfly sat quite still upon the lotus, its wings folded. The sunlight on the water made a brilliant mirror, in which the royal insect was reflected. A gentle wind blew over the lake, causing the lotus to dance upon its root, and the butterfly's rare wings to bend. Chuang's desperate one-arm crawl brought him closer to the floating throne, his long mustaches trailing in the water. With a gasp, the resolute collector raised himself up like a great goose and lunged.

The net swept the air. The butterfly lifted gently off the lotus and hovered for a moment as Chuang sailed past and crashed down beneath the waters of the lake.

"This wretched person is sinking," reflected the collector. Noting that his net was entangled in the roots of the lotus, he surrendered it to the lake, and clambered to the surface. His head broke through the water, into the sunlight. Upon the shore, seated on a blade of grass, was the excellent insect.

Chuang swam the lake and staggered onto the land, covered with water weeds. A snail was fastened to his bald head and a small goldfish flopped in the pocket of his robe.

"Please return to your home, venerable sirs," said Chuang, and bowing, slipped the snail and fish back into the lake. The golden aerialist sat nearby, on the blossom of a cherry tree, fanning its wings.

"You mock this unhappy man, Excellency," moaned the soaking Chuang. "And now that I have sacrificed my net to the jinn of the lake, how am I to catch you?"

The butterfly folded its wings, and contemplated Chuang. Chuang removed his wet robe to dry it in the sun. He looked at the butterfly. "I might have sold you to King Wên," he said, shaking his head. "Wouldn't you like that—a fine glass case to sleep in, touched not by dust nor digested in the stomach of a bird, but mounted for ages in the palace of the Venerable Family?"

Chuang sat upon the ground beneath the cherry tree. "I would not be adverse to such a fate," he said, and lifted his

eyes to the luminous wings peeking over the edge of the cherry blossom. "But of course I have no such splendor to fascinate a king. No," he said, closing his eyes, for his trek through the hills and his plunge in the lake had tired him, "I am nothing but a ruined insect seller."

The sunlight passing through the leaves fell in soft warm beams on Chuang's weary brow. His breathing grew deeper, until soon it was a heavy wind. And as was his habit, he found himself wrapped in darkness.

Who can say how long the darkness lasted? Chuang could not—he had no thoughts, no wishes. He was lost, spun in black thread. A million ages of the king might have passed; or the time of a moth who lives but a single hour.

A crack of light entered Chuang's dark chamber. "Ah," he said, "I have slept and am waking." He stretched, as was his custom on awaking, but found he could not move his arms or legs. "What is this?" he wondered. "Am I still so deep in slumber I cannot rouse my limbs?" He tried once more to rise, and the crack above his head opened slightly, letting in more light.

"But where am I?" he asked himself. "This is most unusual." He struggled to free himself of the blackness and merge with the light. He flexed himself, scratched at the crack, and suddenly his head emerged into the sunlight.

"Well," he said, "I have truly awakened now," and he tried to stand, but could not. He was unable to move his arms and legs. He looked above his head. An enormous white flower hung directly over him. He looked below—he was wrapped in a white cylinder, or trapped, for he still could not move.

"Help!" he cried, but his voice was thin as a thread, and did not echo over the fields. *I must at all costs remove my humble self from this unsatisfying position*, thought Chuang, and with all his might he exercised his limbs, beating at the imprisoning substance, until finally it cracked open completely.

He felt himself free, yet strangely odd in all degrees. Looking down at his feet, he found not flesh and bone, but fiber, thin as a spider's web. He brought his hand to his brow in dismay, only to discover not a hand but a feeler, and instead of a brow of soft skin he encountered a hard-crusted shell.

"Where is my venerable person!" he shouted, clinging fearfully to the twig he found himself upon.

At that moment, he caught sight of a beautiful thin leaf, gold, and covered with indigo dust. "My," he wondered aloud, "what favored tree bears such delicate colors?" He turned to see more, and found the leaf turned with him.

He looked this way and that, and whichever way he turned and looked, there was the leaf. "This is most peculiar," said Chuang. "An exquisite gold leaf seems to have become attached to my ill-favored spine."

Chuang tried to remove the splendid leaf, to let it drop to the ground, but found another, identical to the first, also attached to his spine. The sight of such loveliness, combined with the general cast of the day, which was maddeningly strange, caused him to lose balance and fall from the twig.

He clutched at the sky. "Surely now I've reached the end of my unwholesome career," he said, and shuddered convulsively. An agreeable sensation passed through him, and he hung in mid-air for a moment, before resuming his fall. He shuddered again, this time with conviction, and discovered at once that the gold leaves were his wings, and that he was a butterfly!

The wind was his partner and he floated upon it. He fluttered and dived, rejoicing in the splendor of flight. The field was bright, dazzling with colors. He beat lightly on the air and passed over the myriad flowers and waving grasses, cutting patterns of joy across the field.

Landing upon a white flower shaped like a horn, he rested and watched others like himself fluttering about on ecstatic errands. They drank from the flowers and he too turned inward on the petal, toward the nectar.

He walked down the velvet passage, through which the sunlight passed, into the aroma of the flower's heart. At once intoxicated, he swooned with pleasure, and tasted with his delicate tongue the precious fruit. "O Chuang," he said, "how fortunate you are to have awakened from that unhappy dream of a man, returning at last to your true shape, a prince of the field."

Refreshed immediately by the drink of ambrosia from the flower's heart, he bowed thankfully and backed slowly out. Turning around, he faced the meadow once more. "O perfect day!" he cried, and leapt into space, to dance with his comrades, and chase the numberless smells of delight amidst the constant wave and bending of colors.

Circling the field, he mastered the gentle thrust and balance of his wings, and set out to fly to the mountain treetops. "Now," he exclaimed to himself, "I know why it is called Happiest Meadow." He dove toward a red-petaled jewel-flower, just as a crisscrossing of silk caught him up.

His wings were stuck in threads. He saw the meadow through a silken cage. Suddenly an immensity of hand picked him up by the wings and held him in the air, as a thundering voice said, "For King Wên!"

Into a small, dark box he dropped. He glimpsed the sunlight for a last moment before the lid shut and he was enclosed completely in darkness.

The air was scarce, his tiny heart broken, for he knew Happiest Meadow was gone, and that he was the ephemeral moth doomed to but an hour of life. Folding his wings, he surrendered himself to the black waves.

Who knows how long the butterfly sleeps? For an age—
for an instant? Finally the sun appears.

Chuang woke with a cry upon the shore of the lake, beneath
the cherry-blossom tree, with two legs and two arms and a
head. He rushed to the water and reassured himself with his
reflection. Yes, definitely, he had returned to his former self—
there were his worthless mustaches.

He raised his eyes across the water. The center of the lake
was fluttering brightly, for a flight of butterflies was attending
to a white lotus, in which the King of Butterflies sat, with
folded gold wings.

"Ah, master," cried Chuang across the water, "I shall become
a maker of pots!" And he bowed on bended knee to the radiant
gathering.

In this way did Chuang spend the rest of his days, baking
dishes and cups. His work became so well known he was com-
missioned to produce a set of royal serving plates for the court
of King Wên, which he did, in the pattern of a butterfly, ex-
tremely fine in detail.

Was he a man who dreamt he was a butterfly?

Or a butterfly who dreamt he was a man.

Who knows such things is indeed a dweller in Happiest
Meadow.

THE
FAIRY
KING

THE SNOW WAS crisp and white as John Jingo walked along the mountain path, his lumber ax over his shoulder. He was cutting pine for the Company and the morning was clear and bright, just the kind he liked for swinging an ax in the lonely wood.

The path wound up the mountain. The lumberjack could see his cabin below in the valley, in the snowy pine grove he'd chosen twenty years ago as his home. He'd built the cabin himself, of stone and wood, and it was fine. And today was fine, and every day was fine, when you were your own man in the snow. John Jingo walked along, whistling and slapping his hands together, happy as a man can be.

The leaves were gone from the trees and the mountain was bare, except for the evergreen trees, whose needles stayed on, winter and summer, until they grew old and sick and died. John Jingo cut only the dead trees, for the living trees were his friends. To strike his ax into a still-green tree would be a terrible thing, for he would hear the tree cry out.

So he was just poor John Jingo, who never cut too much

wood, but had a bit of money to buy a new shirt and pants once a year and a pair of strong boots every five. "What more does a man need?" he asked himself, just as a winter robin, fat as a king, rose from the white trail, twittering and winking at him, and landed in the branches of an enormous old oak.

It was the biggest tree John Jingo had ever seen on the mountain. He was surprised he'd never seen it before on this path which he always walked. It was full around as four big men and reached high into the winter sky.

"Good morning, sir," said John Jingo, leaning his ax against the tree. He studied the old bark of the giant, and the acorns growing on its branches, and thought it must be three hundred years old.

He picked up his ax, then, ready to move on, and stepped around the tree. There he saw the opening, large as a door, at the base of the tree—an archway carved, by lightning or what, he knew not, but it was quite large enough to admit a big animal. He approached it cautiously, peering within.

There were steps inside the tree, descending into the earth.

And I have lived here twenty years and not known, thought John Jingo, descending slowly, one step at a time, into the tree's depth.

The stairs curved downward and he followed them without hesitation. Tiny lamps glowing with small fires lit the way, and he knew that it was something very mysterious he'd entered— something beyond the crisp brightness of the winter day, some- thing odd in all respects, weird in every degree, tiny lamps indeed.

The steps were carved out of rock and he took them slowly, spiraling down, one spiral after another, so that he must be approaching the very heart of the mountain, going down, with the flickering lamps to guide him.

The last step at the bottom of the stairway landed John

Jingo in a carved rock hallway, whose gray walls made his heart skip a beat, for he thought that somehow he must have died, and that this was death's chamber, deep in the heart of the earth. He felt his huge bicep with his great hairy hand and decided that he was still the same John Jingo who had walked in the morning up above on the bright path. His breath came out in a mist as he walked down the dark hallway, certain he was still alive.

At the end of the hallway he saw a bright light—of such tremendous intensity he had to halt, for it was not a small lamp but a glowing fire, just beyond the door of the hall. John Jingo gripped his ax firmly and went slowly forward, stepping through the doorway into the vault of the mountain fairies— enormous, golden, covered in jewels.

Amazed, John Jingo stood in the doorway, watching the elfin creatures dance around the great inner theater of the mountain —a bowl, with rings of gold and silver and jade spiraling around it, on which the elegant little creatures played sweet music, in perfect step dancing, round and round toward the bottom of the bowl, where a diamond throne was set, empty and shining.

Above John Jingo's head was another bowl cut in the mountain roof and in it shone star-diamonds and moon-rubies— jewels, thought John Jingo, jewels everywhere. I'm rich!

❊　❊　❊

The vault of the mountain fairies was a great sphere, formed by the two bowls. In this enormous bowl-room, the fairies cavorted around the lumberjack. They were shy toward him, for they were ladies, every one of them tiny, though not too small, and lovely beyond dreams—clad in oak leaves, with miniature wings, in which could be seen thin filmy scenes, changing, of earth's secrets.

John Jingo stood transfixed, leaning on his ax. He was a rough lumberman, with a grizzly beard and the hands of a bear, and he dared not step, for the fairy-girls were so delicately balanced in their dancing he feared to upset them.

He stood, spellbound, for a very long time, content just to look, above and below, at the treasure of fire and diamonds.

The fairies watched him shyly, though finally some fluttered nearer than others, flashing their extraordinary eyes, which sparkled and said to him silently the most unusual things.

John Jingo found himself listening, felt himself filling with fairy-lore, the secrets of old. The fairies whispered of frog-kings and the beginning of things, and of their own birth from acorns many ages ago. John Jingo stood wide-eyed, suddenly wise to the Way of the Fairy and the Cave Gnome, of whom a few were seen amongst the dancers—old fellows, wearing red hoods and carrying pickaxes for the mining of diamonds.

John Jingo found that he knew, by some mysterious magic, their names and origin a thousand ages ago, deep in the early dawn of things. And they knew him too, for they waved and signaled hello with their axes.

"Hello, hello!" called John Jingo, waving his own ax toward the old diggers as he addressed them by name. "Hello, Cabiri, and Bonky, and Spoon, hello, hello!"

The digging gnomes went back to work then, for the fairies were insisting that they dance, and these old fellows were not dancers at all, no, they were diggers.

"I know it all," said John Jingo to himself in wonder. In his hands countless pictures were playing—of lost worlds and dreams, of Star Kings, of the Universal Dragon, of winding caravans through time.

"I thought I was just a dull lumberjack," said John Jingo, beginning a slow walk along the mountain bowl, on a balcony of jade. The fairies made way for him, playing their strings and

drums and flirting with their eyes, sending him songs about the minerals, and their rough stone love—and John Jingo's old ripped suspenders turned into woven jade.

"I am no dull lumberjack," said John Jingo, walking down toward the balcony of gold. "I am a fairy-finder. I am a wise Magician. I am Discoverer of the Lost."

"*Yes*," whispered the fairies, "*that is so.*"

"Glad to have yer with us!" shouted the digging gnomes, tossing diamonds, throwing gold.

John Jingo left the jade balcony, descending four stone steps to the balcony of gold. His hands suddenly became yellow with luster, and etched in them were still more excellent scenes— of gold elephants dancing, of ancient sun-palaces. The cuffs of his lumberjack shirt turned gold, were threaded with gold-embroidered dragons. His baggy lumberjack pants went golden, too, though his suspenders remained in jade.

"My ax!" That old tool was transformed. It had gold head, gold handle, and gold filigree adorned it. "How wonderful," said John Jingo, examining the glorious blade.

"Won't cut nawthin'," said an old gnome named Ed. "Gold's too soft."

"What do I care," cried John Jingo. "I don't have to cut wood any longer, I'm rich!"

"*Yes, yes*," whispered the fairy-women, "*it is yours, take it.*" They brushed him with their wings, sending music through his body, until every one of his muscles was trembling with song— and he, the rough lumberman, turned, like a dancing master, and waltzed with the fairies, round and round, on the balcony of gold.

They danced, through mysterious passages they waltzed, whirling like tops, faster and faster, until they entered the aerial dimension and were spinning in the stars.

John Jingo, Dance Master, danced—from star to star through

the sky. Each star he touched made him grow larger, and he continued to grow, until he was stretched out across the heavens, wondering where else to go, when suddenly—

He was sitting on the diamond throne in the center of the Fairy Bowl, and the stars were diamonds in his crown. His ax-head too had become diamond-edged and he waved it like a royal scepter, saying, "I can cut anything now."

❖　❖　❖

He reigned in the mountain. He was the Fairy King, come in the way that royal fellow always enters his realms—by accident, through the real world above into the dream world below. The fairies served and worshipped him, bringing him fruits and wine of rare vintage, one taste of which brought King Jingo more wisdom, of everything in the forest and the stars.

He married the eldest fairy sister, Jeweliana of Smiles, and she showed King Jingo how to make a pavilion of rubies, simply by wishing correctly, and they lived there many thousands of years, in grand manner.

A child was born to them, a boy of mysterious nature, part magic, part human, able to change himself into a robin. At the age of five hundred years, the magic bird-boy flew off, up the winding stairway, into the world.

King Jingo was naturally concerned, but soon another child was born to them, identical to the first, half magic, half human. King Jingo watched the boy grow, and this time, on the boy's five-hundredth birthday, measures were taken to keep him at home in the bowl. But the boy turned into a robin and escaped in the night, up the mysterious stairway.

King Jingo had twenty sons and lost them all, up the spiraling staircase. His beard grew white and his hair as well and all the magic scenes on his hands and face turned to old things—

old rivers, old bears, old planets, old leaves—and he felt old.

"I know it all," he said to Jeweliana. "I am an old Fairy King."

"*Yes, it is true,*" she said.

"I've had wealth beyond measuring and a soft couch," said the King. "I know the beginning of things."

"*Yes,*" chanted the fairies, gathering around him, "*that is so.*"

"It is time to go," said the King.

"*Oh, no,*" cried Jeweliana, her smile shattering.

"*No,*" cried the fairies, their dancing ceased.

"Yep," said the gnomes, for they knew, they who had been diggers so long, that though the Fairy King reigns a long time, sooner or later, he is through.

"I must know the end of things," said the King, and rising from his diamond throne he walked slowly up the bowl, from balcony to balcony, until his splendid robes changed back to the lumberjack shirt and baggy pants of long ago.

He went to the doorway, waved goodbye with his ax, and entered the hallway, not looking back. He was old, tired, dragged himself along. A light appeared before him, directly in front of the stairs. It was Jeweliana of Smiles, glowing excessively bright.

"*Goodbye,*" she said, and suddenly she was gone, was out, had returned to the ancient and invisible fountain from which her elfin spirit had come.

"It is the end of things," said King Jingo, and sadly he placed his foot on the stairs. They were dust-covered now and growing dark, but as he climbed past the faintly flickering lamps, he felt himself growing stronger, if a bit duller and less wise. As if a gate had closed behind him, he suddenly lost the knowledge of the beginning of things, the secret of the Star Kings, even the face of Jeweliana was vague in his mind; all that was left was a smile.

But he felt solid, and strong, like the old days when first

he'd come down the hole. He cheered up, took the stairs in a rush and leapt out with his old iron ax, into the light.

It was a bright winter's day. There in the snow were his footprints, which he had left—was it an age ago? Or an hour or so? He stood in the lightly falling snow, each flake sparkling like a jewel. What treasure, thought John Jingo, watching the snowflakes fall in his grizzly beard.

He turned back to the old oak. The splendid tree seemed withered, faded, quite dead. He broke off a branch and it snapped, dry and lifeless. The doorway was musty and hung with webs. It was just a hollow, big enough for a porcupine perhaps.

The wind was blowing. A heavy storm was approaching. "I'd best return to my cabin," said John Jingo, and following his old tracks through the snow, he went back down the mountain.

It was the sort of day he liked, with strong wind, bright sun, gray clouds. "I got to dreaming by that old tree, didn't I," he said, walking along, his boots crunching in the snow.

He returned to his cabin and entered, closing the door behind him. There was an old stove, just as he'd left it in the morning, with a few embers remaining. He stirred them up, added some hardwood, and soon the flames were leaping again. He removed his boots and warmed his toes by the glowing iron.

"Was I the Fairy King?"

This question remained with him throughout that day, and all his life, each bright morning as he swung his ax, each night as he sat by the window, watching the stars. When he was an old, gray-bearded logger, and his time had come, he lay in bed, still wondering.

"Just a dream," he said to himself, rolling his old bones over, so that he faced the window and could see the old mountain. "Yes, just a mountain," he thought with a sigh, as he felt himself rising, out of his bed.

Suddenly the sky was filled with the beating of wings. John Jingo raised his head. Toward his cabin came a flight of robins, alighting on his windowsill.

"Come, Father," sang the twenty magic birds through the window, and they and the old lumberjack flew off together, into the hidden dimension, to things that are little known.

THE
OLDEST
MAN

✳❖✳❖✳❖✳❖✳❖✳❖✳❖✳❖

T HOSE TWO WORTHLESS fellows, Kandra and Surya, who liked nothing better than to sit beneath a tree and watch the sky, were doing just that this day, sitting beneath a tree and watching the clouds come and go, like white gods in slow dance.

"Truly, my friend," said Surya, "we have had a good time of it."

"That is so," said Kandra, "for it has been many years since I did a stitch of work."

"I am shocked to hear you say you ever did any," said Surya, who was the older of the two wanderers. "Had I known you were such a foolish fellow, I would not have joined up with you, for I have no wish to be corrupted in my great craft of doing nothing from one end of the day to the other."

"Though it is painful to remember the details," said Kandra, "I seem to be recalling the unfortunate incident."

"Let me hear," said Surya, "the frightening story of how you once did work."

"I was walking through the forest during the season of rain," said Kandra. "A mighty bolt of lightning struck a tree. In order to escape being crushed by the falling trunk, I had to run fifteen steps."

The day passed on. The sun traveled along its highway, and turned down behind the treetops. It was twilight, and the crickets had begun their song, before Surya replied, "A lamentable action. I would not have believed you capable of taking fifteen quick steps to save your worthless hide."

"I am ashamed," said Kandra.

Night fell. Kandra and Surya rose up to walk the moonlit path. They went slow as snails, observing many details of the night missed by more hasty travelers.

They heard the mice prowling the fields, and the footfall of the fox. They were themselves like two old nightbirds with wide eyes, who love the slow passage of the moon-lady over hill and field.

"Ah, my brother," said Kandra, as they walked through a field of wild pumpkin, "who but we know the happiness of thinking nothing and doing nothing? This is the most delightful thing there is, next to sleep."

They sat down in the field and opened a pumpkin, eating out of its rich heart. "Yes, you are right," said Surya, "but I have been giving serious attention to the problem of walking around."

"What do you mean?" asked Kandra.

"Just this," said Surya. "I have spent much energy walking with you from one end of Jambudiva to the other, and it has exhausted me. Though it is true I have never cut so much as a splinter of wood, or touched any of the tools with which men enslave themselves, I have been lifting my two feet for years. I am now ready to put an end to that great waste of effort."

The lady of dawn spread her yellow veil across the hills and fields, waking the flowers. The farmers marched into their fields,

the carpenters raised their hammers, the women began their washing, and Kandra and Surya listened with pain to these various efforts of life all around them.

When the sun was bright overhead, and a great cloud shaped like a chariot had formed on the horizon, something inside Kandra stirred and he said to Surya, "Come, my good fellow, let us do nothing elsewhere. Too long have we tarried in this fine field."

The day came and went, the moon rose again, the mice came out from their holes on soft feet. "There you go again," said Surya, "always rushing about. As for me, I am done with wandering. I declare it, here and now—this field, this position of mine with one leg crossed over the other, hands in my lap, is final. I have walked my last step. Go on without me, though I warn you, all places are the same, and all men fools."

"I am tempted to stay on with you," said Kandra, "but my feet are itching to be gone. I know this indicates great weakness on my part, which undoubtedly results from those fifteen fateful steps I took in the forest to escape being struck by the falling tree."

The stars glittered, faded, died. The sun stirred himself up and dawn came shining, sparkling in the dewdrop mirrors.

"Here," said Surya, "since you are going and I am staying, take this." He dug in his tattered robe and placed a tiny red jewel in Kandra's hand. "It was given to me by the Great Hermit of Nadi, who sat so quietly for so long that ants mistook him for a stone and built their hill around him. It will bring you good luck, but only if you too give it away."

Again the moon came, and when she was on her heights, in the moment when an owl flew across her white face, Kandra put the red jewel in his own tattered robe and knelt before his friend.

"Here," he said, "is a seed from the Mandarava tree, which

lives a million years. They say he who plants it will always have good luck. Since I recognize that you have no wish to spoil your perfect record of never having worked, I plant it for you, here at your feet, and dedicate whatever merit may accrue to my action, to you, Surya, laziest man in creation."

Saying so, Kandra, with great effort, made a tiny hole at the feet of Surya, and planted the Mandarava seed, covering it over with dirt, and watering it with the tears that developed in his eyes due to the strain of performing such a feat of manual labor. It weakened him so much he had to remain until next day, sitting calmly, staring blankly at the sky, before he had the strength to rise up at sunset and be gone.

Kandra wandered then, slowly, as was his style, from village to village, avoiding the places of work, but enjoying the festivals and fairs. He never looked back, but walked straight on, from mountain peak to plain, across the great continent of Jambudiva.

As he was passing through the village of Gaya, a woman came to her doorway, calling, "Hey, tattered one, help me cut some wood, and I'll give you a loaf of bread!"

The Great Loafer watched her out of the corner of his eye, though he carefully avoided turning his head. So terrified was he, he almost took one quick step away from her, but caught himself in time, and continued his slow march out of the village into the welcome cover of the trees.

"Thank goodness, I escaped," he said to himself, but he felt uneasy all day, and consequently walked on and on down the bright forest path, deeper into the wood. The ground was warm beneath his bare feet and he walked for many hours, on a path rarely traveled by men, for it was a deer path, leading through a tangled curtain of leaves, into a shade park known only to animals.

The trees were hung with green moss there, and their twisted roots fell into a small pool, where sunlight came but once a day, for a brief spell. It was now that moment, and as was his custom, a yellow mud turtle who lived in the pool came up from the bottom to greet the sun and sit on a rock.

Kandra sat down in the pebbles along the edge of the pool and watched the wrinkled old turtle taking his sunbath. It was peaceful, as only a forest pool can be, the stillness unbroken save for the cry of a passing bird. Kandra was settling himself for a long afternoon of nothing, when suddenly, out of the trees came an old woman with a sack.

The turtle saw her and dove, but she was fast for her age, and scooped him up, dropping him in her bag.

"Now we'll have some soup!" she cackled, and splashed out of the water, with the sack over her shoulders.

"Wait!" called Kandra.

The old woman turned, startled, and looked at the tattered drifter.

"Please, Mother," said Kandra, "I would speak with you."

"What is it, then," said the old woman. "I'm in a hurry for a hot bowl of turtle soup."

"I want to give you something," said Kandra, and produced the small red jewel given him by Surya.

"What have you got there, dearie?" asked the old woman, walking along the bank toward Kandra.

The little jewel, red as a heart, sparkled in the lone ray of sunshine coming through the forest roof.

"My," said the old woman, "that's a pretty little thing."

"Take it," said Kandra.

"But why?" asked the old woman, picking the stone quickly from Kandra's palm before the fool changed his mind.

"Because its charm works only if it is given away," said Kandra, "and something tells me now is the time."

"Aha," said the old woman, "well, I'll give it to somebody sometime, see if I don't. But," she added, "it won't be good luck for me unless I give you something, dearie," and she dropped her sack, inside of which the turtle scratched, into Kandra's hand. "Now," she said, "the little god of this jewel is truly mine," and away she went, disappearing into the dense forest, by a path known only to herself.

"Well," said Kandra, "the little god of the jewel has performed a good work for you, sir." He opened the sack and let the mud turtle slip out, into the pool. The yellow shell sank down into the dark water and disappeared.

When the shadows of night fell in the forest, Kandra was still sitting by the pool. Soon the moon spilled on the water, like a woman's face rippling with laughter.

Kandra, who spent so much time idly sitting by, found it difficult to tell just when he was sleeping and when he was waking, for the two states blended, one into the other. So, when the yellow turtle suddenly appeared out of the water, and crawled up onto the shore in the moonlight and spoke to him, he was not certain whether it was a dream or a reality.

"Eat this," said the turtle, dropping a yellow root out of his beak onto Kandra's feet, "and you will gain long life."

"How could this be?" asked Kandra, turning the strange yellow root over in his hand.

"I myself have lived since the distant Golden Age," said the turtle, "when all the world was like a newly-opened flower."

All night did Kandra sit in contemplation of the root. Finally, in the gray dawn he ate it, and though finding it somewhat dull in taste he continued eating it throughout his life, which wound on and on, through one century after another.

The old villages fell away, their inhabitants and their descendants disappeared, the stones crumbled, roofs were

covered with vines and swallowed by the jungle, and still Kandra existed and walked on, across the great continent of Jambudiva, from one end to the other.

Great cities crumbled, men's faces changed, still the worthless fellow wandered—though now he was not quite so worthless, having learned so many tongues, even those of birds and animals, to whom he had given close attention over many thousands of years in the forest.

He learned the great secrets of the tiger and the elephant, and the ancient songs of the dove and peacock, passed down through countless generations. They told him how the world had been in the Golden Age, when all the earth was new, like a golden flower, and life was sweet in all degrees.

"All the men were like you," said Ganesha, the Elephant King, "with the secret of long life. But now they have lost and forgotten it, and the Age of Gold is gone."

Kandra had not aged a day since first partaking of the root of eternity. He was now ten thousand years old. His vast, inconceivable memory burned like a sacred fire in his eyes, and kings sought his counsel. From his long experience, Kandra was able to bring many good decisions to bear in royal affairs, though he knew that even so, kingdoms must fall, and fall away, and kings disappear with all their horses and armies.

He continued circling the land slowly, as was his custom, a thousand years here, a thousand there, sometimes sitting beside a stream until that stream had cut a deep gorge in the earth, or perching on a mountaintop to watch generations of eagles in their flight, even once stationing himself in the center of a new village, and sitting so perfectly still that everyone thought him a holy statue and venerated him with flowers. Only after the village had become a great city, and been fought over by rulers, and fallen, and been abandoned, did Kandra rise and stretch his legs.

One nightfall, as he was entering a lovely grove splashed with moonlight, he stepped through a mighty shadow, and looking up, saw above him a giant tree whose branches seemed to climb up to the moon. Turning slowly around, he recognized that very pumpkin field in which he and his long-lost friend Surya had parted.

"And here," cried Kandra, "is the Mandarava, that very great tree itself, which I did plant at his feet! How time has flown, and this tiny seed grown up to the stars. Ah, if only Surya had followed me, instead of staying, he would have learned with me the secret of the golden root, and enjoyed long life, and become the oldest man, beyond the dreams of men."

Sadly then, Kandra sat down at the foot of the great tree, and stared at the fleeting moon, remembering the many good times he'd had with Surya, doing nothing so sweetly in the bygone days. He sat and watched and wondered, and finally the cock crowed, and the sun rose.

"Well," said Kandra, "let me leave this sad place, and see where my footsteps lead." Saying so, he lifted himself up and faced the rising sun.

"Same old Kandra, still with itchy feet."

Kandra spun about, faced the tree, for he was certain a voice had spoken from it, and it was then he saw that the roots he had been sitting on were grown into the shape of crossed legs, and what he thought in the moonlight had been knotholes, were actually the eyes of Surya, the King of Vagrants, enclosed within the trunk of the great Mandarava tree, planted by Kandra so long ago.

THE
ENCHANTED
HORSES

IN A STRAW hut on a mountain lived a painter named Bonovita, famous for his lifelike scenes. Whatever he drew shimmered with life. His painted fruit made the mouth water; he could make anyone's face appear with three strokes of his brush; and viewing his landscapes of mountain, tree, and sky was like looking out a marvelous window.

Now that he was old and no more a part of life in the busy valley below, he was content to remain on his mountain, painting the passing seasons. Spring had just come and the birds had returned with the warm winds and he was painting them. Being old, and having no more to do with the world of men, he had gone deeper into his work, shaping ever more beautiful creatures from his heart and hand—birds of the real world and birds of invisible worlds, so bright and gaily plumed, Bonovita himself cried out with wonder.

One afternoon, as he was completing the wing tip of a bird of paradise, red with the ink of a cherry, he saw a procession coming out of the valley and up the mountainside. His eyes, still keen as an eagle's, made out the great white umbrella of the Queen's palanquin, with woven gold tassels swinging from it.

The tinkling bells of the horses' bridles filled the air, along with the beat of a drum. As the procession wound up the mountainside, Bonovita drew the spectacle in smooth flowing lines, soldiers and horses and umbrella appearing on the paper beneath his flying hands as if by magic.

To his surprise, the splendid caravan stopped in front of his hut and a braided emissary came forward in bright uniform and dark waving mustaches.

"Her Majesty would speak with you, old man," said the soldier.

Bonovita rolled the sketch under his arm, walked over to the veiled platform of the Queen, and bowed low. The white curtains of the palanquin parted and within he saw the Queen, in a blue veil. "Your Majesty," he said, and extended the rolled paper.

"Thank you," said a delicate voice, as a hand smooth and white as ivory came forth to receive the offering.

Though his head was bowed, Bonovita could hear the scroll being unrolled. Then a little gasp within the curtained carriage, as the Queen cried, "Marvelous, sir! It moves before the eyes."

Bonovita longed for a look at her, but the veil hid her face.

"Reverend sir," she said, like a young girl pleading for a sweet, "you must come to the palace and paint a mural in the Golden Gallery."

"Alas, Perfect One," said Bonovita, staring down at the ground, where his bony feet rested in the dust of the path, "though spring has come, the sap no longer rushes in these dried limbs." And he raised his wrinkled arm, but though it was thin and gray, it did not waver.

"We shall carry you," said the Queen, and pointed to an

empty coach behind her own, with blowing veils, and white cushions within.

Bonovita ran his fingers through his tangled beard, as he did whenever he considered a problem of space. He looked down the hillside into the valley where the river flowed in the sun. If I leave my home on the mountain, he thought, I might never return. He looked up to answer no, but the Queen had drawn her veil aside and her face was like the moon, and he could not say no.

The coach was lowered and Bonovita, who had slept for fifty years on a straw mat slung over a board, sank down into the luxurious pillows. "It is too soft," he said to the soldiers. "It will be the end of me." They lifted the coach and away the procession went, down the mountainside, to the palace called Eye-of-the-Sun.

* * *

Bonovita was shown to his quarters in the east wing of the castle, a magnificent room hung with great tapestries of old and attended by many servants. That night, when he climbed into an enormous bed, as into a huge dove's white breast, he longed for his tiny hut, and the streak of moonlight that always came through the open window.

Next day when Bonovita awoke, his servant dressed him in a fiery-red palace robe and served him breakfast on a solid gold table. While he was eating, a man with great ear-whiskers and many medals entered the room.

"Reverend sir," said the ear-whiskered man, bowing to Bonovita, "I am Grand Marshal of the Court. When you are ready, I will show you to the Golden Gallery. All is in readiness for your brush."

Bonovita finished his breakfast of seven precious cereals adorned with glorious fruit, and was led by the Grand Marshal through the stone corridors of the castle. At every doorway two soldiers clicked their heels and raised their swords in salute. Bonovita gave them a little wave of his brush, which he had carried with him from his hut.

"Here, sir," said the Grand Marshal, and they entered a large room. Great gold candle wheels were suspended from the ceiling and the walls were trimmed in gold, except for one wall which was bare. Bonovita's heart leapt—the clear white space of the wall drew him forward. As if in a trance he walked toward it, and figures began to dance in his head, dark and superbly muscled, with black gleaming eyes and flaming hair.

"Horses," he said, stopping at the foot of the wall.

The Grand Marshal left the room quietly and hurried to the King. "Horses," said the Grand Marshal. "Excellent," said the King, who was a devoted horseman.

When the Captain of the King's cavalry received the news he sat up, then stood up, then snapped himself to attention and hurried to the stable, saying to the stableboys, "The horses are to be groomed with special care today."

That afternoon old Bonovita appeared at the stable. He had with him many sketchbooks of the finest pressed paper in the country, provided by the King's architect, and many sticks of lead with which he drew, from every angle, two jet black stallions of the King.

The old painter remained that day and the next, and the next. In fact an entire month did he spend in the stable, sketching day and night, even sleeping there on a pile of hay, which he preferred to his luxurious bed in the castle. Finally, after many sketches, he returned to the Golden Gallery, with brushes he had made in the stable out of horsehair.

He stood before the great white wall of the Golden Gallery, studying every inch of it with great care. He stood there an entire day without moving. The Grand Marshal, looking in, grew concerned, but upon gazing into the old man's eyes, he saw figures mirrored there, as of long ago, half-man, half-horse, galloping.

Finally, at the end of day, in the hour of twilight, Bonovita raised his arm and laid a dark sweeping line upon the wall.

✻ ✻ ✻

The Golden Gallery was closed to all visitors, even the King and Queen, for Bonovita had no wish to be disturbed. He was working as he had not done for forty years—up and down ladders, crouching on a suspended plank, hanging precariously from it, upside down. It must be admitted he found this position good for his circulation. Certainly something was making him feel like a young man again, as if many years had fallen away.

Slowly the horses took form on the wall. Their hooves were high, galloping, their tails long, wild, and free. They ran upon a golden plain, kicking sun dust. Behind them were twisted trees, rising up into a vast blue sky, where rare birds were circling.

Bonovita's princely robe was soon stained a hundred shades of color. So much paint clung to his beard, it looked like a bird's nest made of autumn leaves. The stableboys brought him a bundle of hay to sleep on, and his meals—of rolled oats—which he had grown fond of while sleeping with the horses in the stable.

Day in and day out he shaped the running stallions—looking at them near and far away, laying paint here and there, slowly balancing the movement and the mood. When he went to sleep at night in his bed of hay, he dreamed of horses—silver horses that carried him out the window to the moon—gold horses he rode on to the sun—black horses that galloped down dark underground trails into the fiery heart of the earth.

On certain days, when the weather was cloudy and damp air haunted the castle, Bonovita's old hands grew stiff and he could not hold the brush correctly. On such days he gripped it in his teeth and did light touch-up work on the sky, or around the bark of a tree, or in the delicate grasses.

And on some days he grew sick of horses, and crying "Bah! Horses!" threw his brush on the floor and stamped on it. Then he walked to the window of the castle and looked out, toward his distant beloved mountain.

Months passed, the year fled, still there was no word from the Golden Gallery. The stableboys assured the Grand Marshal that Bonovita was alive. Then one day, the door of the Golden Gallery opened. Bonovita, his robe now a rag of paint, his beard a thousand colors, came forth.

The soldiers saluted the tattered rainbow with alarm. Maids came to every doorway to watch the bent old patchwork shuffle by. The Grand Marshal appeared, and bowing low, inquired of the artist's health.

"Horses," muttered Bonovita, and walked on, through the corridors of the castle, into the courtyard, and down to the stables.

The Cavalry Captain sat up when warned of the old painter's approach, then stood up, then snapped to attention, and marched to the stable. "Yes sir!" he said, giving Bonovita a brisk salute.

The old painter walked into the stable and pointed to the two black stallions. The stableboys quickly bridled them and led them into the courtyard.

The King and Queen, having their morning tea on the balcony overlooking the courtyard, were startled by the appearance of the old man, whom they had not seen for a year. "Is he, perhaps," said the King, "going to sketch the horses in bright sunlight?"

"No," said the Queen, "look!"

Bonovita was holding the door of the palace open, and the stableboys were leading the horses through it, into the castle. The noise of hooves echoed through the corridors.

"Oh, dear," said the Queen.

"Now, now," said the King. "I'm sure the Grand Marshal is in control of the situation."

The Grand Marshal burst onto the balcony. "Horses, Your Majesty," he said excitedly, his ear-whiskers trembling, "walking down the Royal Hallway!"

"Excellent," said the King, and twirling his mustaches, he turned to the Queen. "You see, my dear, everything is under control."

With Bonovita in the lead, and the two stableboys following, the pair of black horses was led through the entire length of the castle, to the door of the Golden Gallery. Bonovita held it open and the stableboys brought the horses inside. Bonovita came in after them and locked the door.

"Can you hold them?" he asked the stableboys.

"Yes sir," said the boys.

"Good," said the old man, and picking up his brush, he began the last touches of his painting. "Now I see," he said, staring first at the two horses and then turning back to his wall. "Horses!"

The horses and the stableboys stayed the night. Though he lay down on his hay, Bonovita did not sleep. The breathing of the horses excited him so, he had to rise again. By the light of a candle, he painted the fire in their dark eyes.

Next morning, a large bale of oats was brought to the Golden Gallery by the cavalry supply officer and Bonovita shared breakfast with the horses. Then he went back to work and painted all morning, all afternoon. Finally, as the sun was

setting behind the great distant mountain, he set down his brushes.

Motioning the stableboys to his side, he took them by the hand and led them over to the painting. Two black horses raced there, hooves shining, nostrils flared, powerful muscles gleaming and tense. In their eyes was a look as wild as the wind, lonely and free, flashing black fire.

"Horses," said Bonovita, and walked out of the room, leaving the door ajar behind him.

The maids, always hovering around for a look at proceedings, sent word through the castle that the painting was finished. Everyone in the palace ran to the Golden Gallery for a look at the masterpiece, and no one saw the old man leave the castle by the stable door, slipping out onto the dusty road that led along the river to the mountain.

*　*　*

That night a brilliant ceremony was held in the Golden Gallery, attended by the courtiers in their finest robes and presided over by the King and Queen. All stood beneath the painting, marveling at the beauty of the scene. There was music, food, and dancing in the Golden Gallery, but every eye kept returning to the painting, to the dark horses, who seemed ready to spring off the wall. When midnight came, the room was emptied, and guards were posted at the door.

Toward the dawn, the clatter of galloping hooves was heard in the sleeping castle. The guards summoned the Captain of Cavalry from his dreams, claiming that two fierce shadows had brushed past them at the door of the Golden Gallery, nearly knocking them down. The Captain sat up in bed, then stood up, then snapped to attention in his pajamas. "Investigate at once," he said, and he and his men ran outside into the court-

yard. The grass, wet with dew, appeared to have been trampled upon.

"Quick!" said the Captain, and all raced to the Golden Gallery.

The Grand Marshal came in his nightcap, for he was the one who held the key to the Golden Gallery. He removed it from the cord around his neck and put it in the lock. The door opened and the men pushed through. The Captain ran to the wall and let out a cry.

"What is it?" asked the Grand Marshal, rushing to the wall, where he saw, shivering back into place on the painted field, the black stallions, their bodies wet with dew.

*　*　*

Every night it was the same—hoofbeats down the hall, the trampled grass, and the gatekeeper's familiar story of two mysterious shadows leaping the palace wall into the open valley.

The villagers told a tale too, of galloping shadows along the river, and the lonely shepherds of the mountain claimed that every night ghostly horses raced up the mountain to the shack of Bonovita, neighing and whinnying outside his door, until he came out to them and stroked their necks and whispered in their ears. Only then would they turn around and go back down the mountain into the valley and along the river to the castle, leaping the palace gates and returning into place on the wall, hides foaming from their run.

One night everyone in the valley and the castle saw the two black horses glistening in the moonlit sky, pulling a golden coach, in which old Bonovita rode, smiling.

"What has happened?" cried the King from his balcony, to the shepherds entering the courtyard below.

"Bonovita has died."

For six days and nights the horses were gone, and all that remained of them in the painting was a white space.

The King and Grand Marshal kept constant vigil. On the seventh night, there was a rushing wind at the window, and two shadows leapt into the Golden Gallery.

"Your Majesty, look!" cried the Grand Marshal.

The shining black horses were trembling back into place on the wall, and their manes had turned snow white.

HEARTS OF WOOD

was set by Maryland Linotype Composition Co., in linotype Caledonia, a typeface designed by the great American calligrapher and graphic artist W.A. Dwiggins. This clear and classic face was inspired by the work of Scotch typefounders, and particularly by the transitional faces cut by William Martin for Bulmer around 1790.

The book has been printed and bound by Alpine Press, Stoughton, MA. Book design by Virginia Evans.